Cle

KT-444-360

For my squad – DaveTheRave,
Meik and Whymars
– Tom
For Garys (and their dads)
all over the universe
– Anjan

STRIPES PUBLISHING LTD
An imprint of the Little Tiger Group
1 Coda Studios, 189 Munster Road,
London SW6 6AW

A paperback original
First published in Great Britain in 2019

Text copyright © Tom Nicoll, 2019
Illustrations copyright © Anjan Sarkar, 2019

ISBN: 978-1-78895-071-8

A CIP catalogue record for this book is available
from the British Library.

Printed and bound in the UK.

2 4 6 8 10 9 7 5 3 1

TOM NICOLL

LEVEL UP!

ILLUSTRATED BY
ANJAN SARKAR

Stripes

LEVEL 1

"Are you sure we should be doing this?" whispered Max as we tiptoed into my mum's workshop. The place was littered with all kinds of junk – broken electronics, piles of circuit boards and brightly coloured wires snaking all over the place. We had to take great care not to trip over Mum's half-finished projects.

"Yeah, of course," I said, stepping over the remains of a toaster. "Why?"

"It's just that we're talking really quietly and tiptoeing about," he said. "Which doesn't usually mean that we're allowed to do something. Also, there's a cardboard sign over there that says *Don't even think about it, Flo.*"

"There is not..." I said, before spotting the sign myself. It was propped up against a bulky metal device, with what looked like part of an eyepiece peeking out from behind it. I gave Max a reassuring laugh. "Oh, that's just Mum's sense of humour. You know what scientists are like. She's always leaving daft signs around. *Don't leave the fridge door open, Flo* or *Don't forget to wash your hands after going to the toilet, Flo.* Honestly, you shouldn't take her seriously."

Max frowned. "You don't wash your hands?"

"Of course I do," I said, rolling my eyes. "But she wants me to do it *every* time. I'm not the blinking Queen, am I?"

"Well ... no..." admitted Max. "But..."

"Exactly. Besides, have I ever led you astray?"

"All the time," he said, nodding vigorously. "Pretty much every day of my life."

"*Every* day?" I repeated doubtfully.

"Fine, not *every* day," he conceded. "You did go on holiday for a week last year, so..."

"Ugh, you're such an exaggerator. Let's just take a look at this machine and then we can go," I said, grabbing the sign and flinging it away. But behind it was another piece of card that read, *I'm serious, Flo. Under no circumstances should you touch this device until I tell you it's ready.*

"What a joker," I said, flinging that one away too. There were another couple of signs after that, but I didn't even bother reading those. "What have we got, then?"

It was a metal box about the size of my head. Sticking out of the top was a pair of black goggles, with what looked like a chin rest underneath them. A cable at the back of the box was connected to my mum's computer, which was currently powered down.

"Looks like one of those machines opticians use,"
I said. "The ones that blow air into your eyes to test
if you can keep them open when it's windy."

"That's to test for glaucoma," Max pointed out,
pushing his specs up his nose.

"This machine *definitely* doesn't do that," I said.
"Hardly anyone I know has got one. Only that
puffed-up poser Rhett Hodges."

Max nodded. "Great," he said, without much
enthusiasm. "Sounds good."

"You have no idea what it is, do you?" I said.

"None whatsoever," he admitted.

I let out a groan. "You know Hodges, right? The
older kid from school?"

"Yeah," sighed Max. "You never stop going on
about him. He's like the biggest game streamer in
the country or something. And he always beats

you at video games."

I could feel my face go bright red. "He does not always beat me!" I snapped.

"Shhh!" said Max. "Your mum might hear us."

"Fine, but he doesn't *always* beat me at video games," I said. "Besides, he only ever plays *Star Smasher*. Well, used to play it anyway. He stopped streaming after I finally beat him. Though conveniently his stream cut out right before anyone could see it happen."

"Yeah, that was convenient..." said Max, letting the thought trail off.

"Are you saying I'm making it up?" I put my hands on my hips.

Max fell silent.

"People thought he was great because he was able to buy amazing equipment with all the money he got from streaming," I said. "If Mum would just let me start my own stream then maybe I'd be able to buy a DIS too."

Max scratched his chin. "A DIS?"

"A Digital Imprint Scanner," I said. "They've just come out and they're amazing. Basically they scan your DNA and turn it into computer code."

Max continued to scratch his chin. "I see. What for, exactly?"

Max didn't really get computers and games the way I did. Sometimes things that seemed perfectly obvious to me, he just didn't have a clue about. It was like talking to most grown-ups.

"Imagine being able to see yourself in any video game ever made," I said. "That's what the device does. Some games come with editors that let you change how your avatar looks, so maybe after a few hours of changing gazillions of body parts, you finally end up with someone who kind of looks like you if you squint really hard. But this thing does all the work for you. For *any* game. Even ones that wouldn't normally let you change your character. It's amazing. But it's also super expensive."

Max looked at the device sitting on the table. "Your mum bought you one?"

I shook my head. "Mum's a scientist for the government, remember," I said. "She can't afford to buy me one. But when I told her about it, she got pretty excited. She figured she could build one herself. The problem is she won't let me use it until it's ready."

"That's probably sensible, isn't it?" asked Max.

Not only did he not get video games, Max didn't get my mum. "No," I said firmly. "You don't understand. I mean, don't get me wrong, Mum is a genius. But the problem is she never finishes anything. Look around you. She starts building all these cool things, but she never completes them. She just keeps tinkering with them until she has a new idea, then switches to that. I'll be waiting forever for her to finish this."

Max didn't look convinced. "I don't know, Flo, I think you should probably hold off..."

Ignoring him, I switched on Mum's computer, which was lightning-fast. She'd fitted it with loads of upgrades – tons of memory, a cutting-edge graphics card and a solid-state hard drive. It was great for playing games on.

It only took a few seconds to fire up. When it did, instead of the usual login screen, I was presented with a text prompt:

```
>BOOT UP FLO-SCAN OS V0.01? Y/N
```

"Flo-scan?" I said, smiling. "She named it after me. Cool!" I pressed the *Y* key and watched as a bunch of ones and zeros scrolled up the screen. After a few moments, a green light flickered on the front of the device that was connected to the computer, accompanied by a strange whirring noise. On screen, the numbers disappeared, replaced by another prompt:

```
>WHEN READY, PLEASE PLACE CHIN
ON THE REST AND LOOK DIRECTLY
INTO THE LENS
```

"Right, here goes," I said. Pressing my chin against the plastic, I looked right into the eyepiece and...

Nothing.

"Why's it not doing anything?" I asked.

"That's odd. It's like it's not finished," said Max sarcastically.

I raised my head and looked at the screen again.

"It looks pretty cool, though," said Max, clearly trying to make me feel better. He placed his own chin on the rest. "I'm sure it'll be great when it's ready."

"Maybe you need to do something else," I muttered to myself, looking down at the keyboard. I pushed the *Enter* key.

```
>INITIATING SCAN...
>>SCAN COMPLETE
```

I stared at the monitor. "Is that it?"

I turned to Max.

Or rather, I turned to where Max had been.

He was no longer there.

"Max?" I said, looking around. But there was no

sign of him. "Very funny. Knock it off! Seriously.

Where are you?"

I had a sinking feeling. Max wasn't the type of

person to play practical jokes. In fact, Max hated

pranks of all kinds. He told me as much every time

I pulled one on him. Which, to be fair, was quite

often.

I looked curiously at the device.

Mum had told me it wasn't ready. But had she

meant it wasn't ready like when she hadn't finished

cooking my dinner, or did she mean it wasn't ready like when she hadn't finished ironing my school clothes. Because food poisoning isn't fun, but I could happily live with creases in my uniform.

There was only one way to find out. I looked into the eyepiece and pressed the *Enter* key.

*

I was on the Moon. Or at the very least I was on *a* moon. The ground was grey and hard and there were craters everywhere. Instead of a roof or even a sky, above me was just the blackness of outer space, dotted with countless shimmering stars.

Max was here too. At least, it looked like him. He had on the same blue jeans and green hoodie but they looked fuzzier somehow. In fact, nothing about him was as sharp as before. I looked down at my arms and those didn't seem right either. My red dress was flat and rigid, as if it was made from cardboard instead of cloth.

"Flo!" Max cried. "What's going on? Where are we?"

Before I could even respond, a laser bolt struck Max in the chest, and he vanished.

LEVEL 2

"Max!" I screamed into the empty space where he had been standing.

"Yeah?" he said.

His sudden reappearance almost caused me to stumble backwards into a large crater

"Wait... Max... You're alive?" I asked, steadying myself.

"Well, yeah," he said, looking at me like I'd just stated the most obvious thing in the world.

"But you were shot. With a laser. You disappeared."

"Shot?" he repeated. "A laser? Disappeared?"

"Yes!"

"That doesn't sound very likely," he said, before another laser struck him in the head, obliterating him for a second time. Moments later, he reappeared in the exact same spot.

"See!" I said. "It just happened again."

"Right, yeah, I noticed it that time!" he replied. "But where's it coming from?"

"Probably that tank over there," I said, pointing into the distance over his shoulder. "Or maybe it came from one of those other tanks behind that tank that are shooting lasers at all the other tanks. But, safe to say, it's from a tank."

"Flo?"

"Yes, Max?"

"Why are we on a moon with lots of tanks

shooting lasers at each other?"

Good question. This was all so familiar. I'd seen it somewhere before. And then I remembered. "Max, this is going to sound crazy, but..."

Another laser blast disintegrated him.

"Sorry," he said after reappearing. "What were you saying?"

"I think we're inside a video game," I said, trying to contain my excitement.

Max paused for a second. "You're right," he agreed. "That does sound crazy."

"But it's true!" I argued. "This is the opening level of *Star Smasher*! Those are Space Tanks. And there are real people controlling them, trying to blow each other up."

"Why?" asked Max.

"Why what?"

"Why are they trying to blow each other up?" asked Max.

"Because ... because ... that's the game," I said. "Part of it anyway."

Max just shook his head. "I really don't understand the appeal of these types of games," he said. "I mean, wouldn't it make more sense for them to talk through their problems, instead of—" He broke off as he was blasted by another laser.

"Getting fed up of that," he said after respawning.

"If it's any consolation, I think it's just stray blasts," I said. "I don't think anyone's actually aiming at you."

"No, it's no consolation at all," said Max. "And how come none are hitting you?"

I shrugged.

Max folded his arms in annoyance. "How is any of this even possible?" he asked.

"It must have been Mum's machine," I said. "And you can wipe that 'I told you so' look off your face. How was I meant to know this would happen? It's Mum's fault really. She could have at least left a warning that her machine wasn't ready yet."

"SHE LEFT YOU LOADS!" yelled Max. "YOU THREW THEM ALL AWAY!"

"That doesn't sound like me," I said.

Max just rolled his eyes and sighed. "Now what do we do?" he asked. "I'd rather not stand about and get blown up all day, if it's all the same to you."

"We need to get one of those tanks," I said.

"How are we going to do that?" asked Max.

I looked around the barren moon surface. I'd seen this landscape countless times while playing the game, but now actually being *in* the game, it was like discovering everything for the first time. It was incredible – as if we were on a real moon. Unfortunately, like a real moon, there wasn't much of anything, let alone something that could help us steal a tank. Except for... I put two fingers in my mouth and made a piercing whistle.

All the tanks in the distance stopped dead in their tracks.

Players of *Star Smasher* were used to lots of

different sounds, including (but not limited to):

> - Explosions.
> - The pow-pow of lasers.
> - The roar of tank and spaceship engines.
> - Chatter from the NPCs (Non-Player Characters).
> - Other players (mostly) insulting them over Voice Chat.

They weren't used to someone whistling to get their attention. Every gun turret turned towards us.

"Um... Flo, what you doing?" asked Max nervously, as I started waving at the tanks. "They're going to blow us to the moon. I mean ... ANOTHER moon!"

I shook my head. "No, they're not," I said. "Trust me. There's only one thing more fun to do in a video game tank than blow stuff up."

One of the tanks broke away from the others and

began trundling towards us.

"You can't mean...?" said Max.

"Yep."

"Look, I'll admit I'm not an expert in video games like you are, Flo," said Max, as the tank sped up. "But ... how does us getting squashed by a tank help matters?"

"Just wait," I told him, grabbing him by the arm. The tank was approaching at full speed now. It would crush us in seconds. My heart was pounding.

"Flo?" said Max. "Flo, we have to go. Flo!"

"Three..." I said.

"Flo, come on!"

"Two..."

"FLO!"

"One..."

As the tank was about to strike us I took a single

step backwards, still gripping Max's arm, and the two of us tumbled into the crater behind. We hit the ground just in time to watch as the tank flew overhead, its front dipping in mid-air, causing it to flip over and smash down into the crater beside us.

It lay motionless on its back for a few seconds, just metres away. Then suddenly its tracks started spinning again, as if this had any chance of helping. After about half a minute, they went still.

"A little help here?" came a boy's voice from inside the tank.

"You tried to run us over!" I said.

"Um ... no I didn't," said the boy. "I was ... seeing if you wanted a lift."

"Yeah, right," muttered Max.

"Come on," pleaded the boy. "Look, just tell me the command to flip the tank. I'm new at this."

"You promise you won't try to run us over or blow us up any more?" I asked.

"Promise!" said the boy.

"All right," I said. "Press *ALT-F4*."

"Ha ha, suckers!" cried the boy.

There was a flicker, then the words

"**rudeboy90210 has logged off**" appeared in

large green letters, floating above the tank, before

quickly fading away.

Video Game Tip: ALT-F4 is a handy keyboard shortcut for immediately quitting the current game. Less handy when trying to flip tanks.

"Right, that's him gone," I said. "Now we have a

tank."

"Yeah, but an upside-down one," Max pointed out.

"How are we going to get it the right way up?"

"Easy," I said.

Video Game Tip: Press X to flip a tank. X. Not ALT-F4

While I couldn't press *X*, not having a controller

and all, I'd played enough video games to know that

while pressing *X* might make any number of things

happen – from opening a door to petting a dog –

usually your character just reached out and touched something. So that's exactly what I did. I pressed a hand lightly against the side of the tank, then watched as it flipped itself upright.

"Woah!" said Max.

I jumped on top of the tank, pulled open the hatch and climbed inside. There wasn't much room inside the cockpit, a situation that wasn't helped by Max clambering in next to me moments later. Thankfully the controls weren't as complicated as a real tank's. A little controller, like the ones for an Xbox or PlayStation, dangled from a cord. Seconds later, Max and I were rolling out of the crater and towards the action.

"Why are we heading towards the other tanks?" asked a panicked Max. "Shouldn't we try to find a way out of the game?"

"I don't see a door out of here," I said. "Do you?"

"Um ... no."

"In my experience, there's only one way a video game ends," I said. "And that's by completing it."

"In my experience they usually end with me dying over and over," said Max.

"We *could* try that if you think it'll help?" I said, grinning.

Max sighed. "No, let's go with your idea."

LEVEL 3

"Take that," I said, before blasting a tank into orbit. I turned towards another and let off a volley of lasers at it. "Oh, don't worry, I haven't forgotten about you."

"Flo," said Max. "We've been blowing up tanks for ages now. How exactly do you win this game, then? Is this it?"

"This?" I said, pulling off a sharp handbrake turn, causing two tanks to smash into each other. "Oh no. This is just an opening mission. *Star Smasher* is an open-world MMORPG."

Max screwed up his face. "A what?"

"A Massively Multiplayer Online Role-Playing Game," I said, firing another direct hit. "Thousands of people in different places playing the same game. There's an overall story to complete, but there are hundreds of different missions you can do along the way. This is the first one. You win space credits for blowing up the other tanks and then when you've saved up enough you can buy a ship to go off and explore the galaxy."

"So, do we have enough credits yet?" Max asked.

I blurted out a laugh. "Good one," I said, before noticing Max's confused expression. "Oh, you're serious? No. It takes about a week to scrape together enough. And that's if you're as good at the game as me, which no one is. Seriously, this game is like a full-time job sometimes."

"A WEEK?" shouted Max. "We can't sit inside a tank inside a video game for a week. We need to complete the game now."

"I mean, that's just to get a ship," I continued. "To actually complete the game, you have to enrol in the Imperial Fleet, work your way up the ranks, earn the trust of the Emperor, gain a position on board his personal transport ship, the *Phoenix*, and destroy the Resurrection Gem – a stone forged from the embers of a dead star that grants the Emperor the ability to bring himself and his troops back from the dead. That can take about half a year. And that's if you're in a hurry."

Max looked like he was about to cry.

"Look, I'm not that thrilled by the idea either," I said, "even though this is a lot of fun. But it's just how the game works. I mean, it's not like we could just steal the next ship we see. Like that one over there."

Some way off in the distance, a spacecraft was about to touch down on the moon's surface. It was hard to be sure, but to me it looked like a small military transport ship.

"Why not?" asked Max.

"Why not what?" I said.

"Why can't we steal it?" said Max. "I mean, we do have a tank. We could steal the ship and fly straight to the *Phoenix*."

"Max, I like your spirit," I said as I blasted another couple of tanks. "But we can't do that because the game doesn't let you."

"How do you know?" asked Max. "I'm pretty sure the game doesn't allow real humans to wander about in it, yet here we are. What have we got to lose by trying?"

He had a point. "You're right," I said. "Though there is one other problem."

Max groaned. "What?"

"Maybe you haven't noticed, but this part of the moon is surrounded by a giant trench. And that ship is on the other side. We have no way to get over to it."

Max said nothing for a few moments. He just stared out of the window, rubbing his chin. Suddenly his face lit up. "I've got it," he said. "We're on a moon. Gravity works differently on a moon, right? If we went fast enough, could we jump it?"

I shook my head. "Nice idea," I said. "But the

makers of the game didn't bother with realistic gravity. The only way you'd be able to jump that distance in this game is... Oh, Max, you're a genius!"

"I am?" said Max.

I spun the tank so it was pointing towards the ship then accelerated forwards, quickly leaving the other tanks behind.

Suddenly there was a boom behind us, louder than anything we'd heard since arriving.

"What was that?" asked Max.

I kept the tank accelerating away from the fighting but turned the turret round to see what was happening. There were more loud booms as tank after tank was taken out rapidly.

"Looks like we left just in time," said Max. "What is it?"

"Another player," I said, before turning the turret

back round. "A good one by the looks of it. We don't have time to worry about that now, though. This is going to take my full concentration."

"What are you planning?" asked Max, nervousness creeping into his voice.

"A rocket jump," I said.

"What's a rocket jump?" asked Max.

Video Game Tip: A rocket jump is a video game technique enabling you to jump great distances by firing a rocket at your feet and using the force of the explosion to propel you further through the air. In case it needs to be said, this won't work in real life, so please don't try it at home.

"It's probably best you don't know," I said.

The other thing was, I had no idea if this was going to work. A rocket jump normally involved

a) a rocket launcher and b) someone who could jump. What I was about to try didn't involve either of those things.

"Hang on," said Max, as something seemed to occur to him. "A rocket jump? Is that what it sounds like? Flo, surely you're not thinking..."

As we neared the edge of the trench, travelling faster than a blue hedgehog in a hurry, I spotted the thing I'd need if I was going to pull this off. At full speed, I clipped the edge of a small crater. The force was enough to flip the tank forwards into the air. When the turret of the cannon was directly above the surface of the moon, I pulled the trigger.

BOOOOM!

The explosion sent the tank soaring into the air, rotating furiously like an out-of-control fidget spinner. We bounced around for ages, until finally the tank landed with an almighty crash.

"Max ... you OK?" I asked, aware that the world was currently on its side.

"That depends," said Max. "What exactly do you mean by OK?"

"Still alive, I guess."

"Oh," said Max. "Then yeah, I'm OK."

Suddenly the inside of the tank started to flash red.

"What's happening now?" asked Max.

"That means the tank is about to explode," I said.

"Oh, brilliant."

"Come on," I said, crawling towards the hatch. I tried to open it but it wouldn't budge. I turned on my back and tried kicking it a few times, but that didn't help either.

"Are we trapped?" cried a panic-stricken Max.

"Er … well…" I began, before having a brainwave. "Oh, I know! Max, the controller. Press the yellow button."

Max reached out and pressed the button. The hatch door swung open.

"Let's move!" I yelled, scrambling out of the ready-to-explode tank. Once I was free, I reached in to help pull Max out. We tumbled to the ground just in time to watch the vehicle go boom.

I stood up and casually dusted myself down. "So, that was fun," I said. "Now let's see about stealing this ship."

"Er … Flo?" said Max.

"Yeah?"

"I think they might have something to say about that," said Max, pointing off to the left. Several giant heavily armoured figures were marching towards us, their laser cannons aimed in our direction.

LEVEL 4

There were eight figures in total, each kitted out in green and silver power armour and wielding laser cannons that were almost as big as us. I recognized them immediately as Space Soldiers, part of the elite army of the Emperor. Since the aim of the game was to overthrow the Emperor, the Space Soldiers were not typically friendly. I was also right about the ship they had arrived in. It was a Class-C Model X-2500 Lightbringer, one of the smaller Empire transport ships, but one usually reserved for royalty or higher-ranking officers. Which meant there was probably someone pretty important here...

"Now what?" whispered Max.

"I don't know," I said, frowning. "If I had a laser cannon of my own, I'd just blast these giant knuckleheads to smithereens and take their ship."

"Can't we try reasoning with them?" asked Max. "They might be willing to help us."

I gave Max a withering look. "Of course not," I said. "These are just mindless bots with a few pre-programmed phrases and actions. But even if they weren't, they're part of the Empire. They're ruthless and cruel and wouldn't help you even if you paid them. Big, dumb and evil, that's them."

The Space Soldiers exchanged looks. "You do know we can hear you, right?" said one of them. She pressed a button on the side of her helmet and the middle part slid up, revealing an annoyed-looking woman.

"Hang on," I said, looking at her quizzically. "You mean you can understand me?"

"Yes," she replied. "Not bad for big, dumb, evil Space Soldiers, huh?"

"This is unbelievable," I said.

"Not as unbelievable as someone rocket-jumping a tank across the gorge," she said. "And you call *us* mindless."

"We had to," said Max. "You see..."

It was then that the door to the transport ship opened. Out stepped another Space Soldier. This one had no helmet and he looked exactly like characters usually looked in these kinds of games – a blond quiff, a mean but handsome face and a stubble-covered chin the size of a cement block.

"Well done, Captain Moretta," shouted the man, as the woman saluted him. "The Red Ghost! Caught at last. Not bad."

I looked down at my red dress. "Ghost?" I repeated.

"Your reign of terror over the citizens of the Empire has come to an end," declared the chisel-jawed man. "For truly, you were no match for me, Commander Gary Orioncloud, son of Emperor Horatio Orioncloud…"

"*Gary?*" I interrupted. "That's your name? Gary?"

Commander Gary looked more than a little confused. "Er … yes. Why?"

"It's not your typical giant Space Soldier name, is it?" agreed Max.

"Exactly," I said. "I mean, your dad on the other hand. Horatio. Now *that's* a Space Soldier name."

Gary's cheeks looked like they were burning. "There's nothing wrong with *Gary*. It's a very noble name. Not that I would expect the Red Ghost to know anything about nobility."

"I'm NOT the Red Ghost," I said, rolling my eyes. "My name is Flo. And this is my friend Max. We're just trying to get home."

"A likely story," declared Gary.

"Your Highness," said Captain Moretta, pointing towards the other side of the gorge. "She may be telling the truth. Someone over there is lighting the place up."

"Oh, that," I said. "Yeah, some new tank showed up just before we left. They were making short work of the others from what we saw. Even I don't move that fast. It wouldn't surprise me if they're cheating."

"We should investigate," said Captain Moretta. "It may be the real Red Ghost."

Gary laughed feebly. "Come on now, Alice. We've got the real Red Ghost right here."

"But what if she's not?" protested Moretta.

"She is!" said Gary. "I mean, look, she's dressed in red. She rocket-jumps tanks. What more proof do you need?"

"We should be sure," Moretta said, refusing to back down.

Gary's face started twitching as he looked across the gorge. Every second or so a little flash went off, indicating another tank had bitten the dust. "OK, look, why don't you take the rest of the squad and investigate while I personally escort the Red Ghost and her sidekick to the Imperial Jail."

"Jail?" I said.

"Sidekick?" said Max.

"You're going to take the ship?" protested Captain Moretta, looking about as happy as we were at the situation.

"Oh, don't worry about me," said Gary. "I'm more than a match for these two."

"No, that's not what I meant—" she replied.

"Of course, I'll arrange for another ship to come

and extract you," Gary interrupted. "But it's of utmost importance that we get these two behind bars as quickly as possible."

"With all due respect, Your Highness," said Moretta, reminding me very much of the times my mum was close to losing all patience with me, "the Emperor will be furious if we let you return unaccompanied. What if something were to happen to you?"

Gary waved her off. "Don't you worry about Dad," he said. "He made me Commander, and that's exactly what I'm doing. Commanding. Captain Moretta, I command you to ... you know ... do all the things I just said. Um ... please."

Captain Moretta let out a sigh before holstering her laser cannon on to her back. She then reached into a small compartment on her hip and took out a pair of handcuffs. Before I could react, she had snapped them shut round my wrists.

"Hey!" I objected as she did the same to Max.

"You remember the route back to the *Phoenix*?" Moretta asked Gary.

"Yes, *of course*," said Gary, rolling his eyes.

Captain Moretta frowned. "It's just … you did spend the entire trip here reciting lines for a play. It didn't seem like you were paying that much attention."

"I'm an excellent multi-tasker, Alice," he said. "Even while we've been speaking I've thought of three whole new ideas for plays. No, wait – four!"

"Head towards the Commodore LXIV system," said Moretta, ignoring him. "Then take a left when you reach Vic XX. You'll eventually meet up with the fleet. Don't go right or you'll wind up in the Combat Zones."

"Commodore ... Vic ... got it," said Gary. "Come on then, you two, get on board."

Moments later, Max and I were sitting on board the Lightbringer. From the windows we could see Moretta and the rest of Gary's squad shaking their heads in disbelief before they faded from our view as the ship rocketed towards the stars.

LEVEL 5

The inside of the Lightbringer was pretty
impressive. It had smooth, curved white walls, a
spotless silver floor and a cockpit made entirely of
glass. It was as if someone had taken the first-class
section of an aeroplane and combined it with a
submarine. As the ship didn't have a prisoner hold,
Max and I were up near the front in the passenger
seating.

"Oh, man, Dad's going to be so happy with me
capturing you both," said Gary, leaning back in
the pilot's chair and putting his feet up on the

dashboard. "With any luck he'll be so pleased he won't send me out on any more missions."

Gary reached for a microphone. "This is Commander Gary Orioncloud. I am en route to the *Phoenix* with the Red Ghost. Repeat, I am en route with the Red Ghost. Let my dad know, will you? Oh, and send a transport ship to my last landing position to pick up my squad. Over."

"Roger that," came a voice at the other end. "Well done, Your Highness. Over."

"Look, how many times do I have to tell you? I'm NOT the Red Ghost," I said.

Gary hung up the mic then tapped his nose, giving us a knowing look. "That's exactly the sort of thing the Red Ghost would say, though, isn't it?"

Max and I both groaned.

"This is hopeless," said Max.

I didn't want to agree but it was definitely beginning to look like things couldn't get much worse.

"Hey, we've got some time to kill," said Gary. "Why don't I give you an exclusive preview of my upcoming one-man play entitled *His Father's Son*?"

OK, so I was wrong. Things could get much worse.

"... and that is why, Father, I do not want to be a Space Soldier any more. The end."

After what felt like hours, but might have only been minutes, the show finished and Gary took a bow.

Max and I clapped half-heartedly, mostly out of relief it was over, partly because of the handcuffs.

"Thank you, thank you," said Gary, lapping it up. "Thanks for being such a captive audience. *Captive*, get it? Just a little Space-Soldier-actor humour there for you. Seriously, though, what did you think?"

I only a managed a shrug, but Max said, "It sounds like you have a lot of issues with your father."

"I ... I don't know what you mean," said Gary.

"The entire play is about a soldier, whose dad is

the king," explained Max. "But the soldier doesn't like being a soldier and wants to be a singer instead. It's obviously about you. Have you tried telling your dad any of this?"

Gary looked a bit sheepish, and forced a laugh. "Ha! Obviously it isn't about me. For one thing, my dad is the Emperor, not a king. And two, I'm a *Space* Soldier, not a soldier. And three, I want to be an actor, not a singer... Though I do have incredible range... Oh, wait, we're at Vic XX. Now, which way did Captain Moretta say again? Was it left or right?"

"Left," I said.

"Yeah, left," agreed Max.

"Cool, thanks," said Gary. He started pulling the flight stick to the left, before stopping abruptly. He smirked at us. "Yeah. Nice try. As if I'm stupid enough to take directions from you."

Gary pulled the stick in the other direction, spinning the ship round to the right.

"No!" I shouted. "You're going to fly us into the Combat Zones!"

"As if," Gary scoffed.

About a minute later, we saw the first of the ships.

"Ah, there we are," said Gary. "The Imperial Fleet, out to welcome us, no doubt."

"Do the Imperial Fleet always shoot at each other?" asked Max.

Gary's face turned as white as the ship's interior.

"We told you to go left," I pointed out

"But ... but ... I thought," said Gary.

"Well, you thought wrong," I said. "Maybe if you'd listened to us at the start when I told you I'M NOT THE RED GHOST we wouldn't be in this situation!"

Gary swallowed. You could actually hear the huge

lump in his throat. "I need to turn round," he said,

slamming the flight stick to the left.

But it was too late. Ships were all around us.

"Mayday, Mayday!" Gary shouted into the microphone. "Your beloved Commander Gary is under attack! Please send all available fighters to assist. In fact, send the unavailable ones too."

There was no response. Suddenly the ship shuddered, almost knocking us out of our seats.

"We've been hit!" cried Gary. "Oh no! This is terrible. What are we going to do?"

"Oh, it's 'we' now, is it?" I muttered.

"Gary, you've got to let us out of these handcuffs," said Max.

"What?" said Gary.

"Flo's a brilliant pilot, she can get us through this," said Max. "Right, Flo?"

"That's true, I am brilliant," I agreed modestly.

A terrified Gary looked from the window to us and back again, unsure what to do. Another blast rocked the ship, causing red lights to start flashing.

"All right, all right," he said, taking out his laser cannon. "Moretta has the keys," he added, seeing the alarmed looks on our faces. He pointed the cannon at the handcuffs and blew them apart. First mine, then Max's.

I stood up, keeping a tight hold of my chair as the ship thrashed around, but didn't move any further.

"What are you waiting for?" yelled Gary.

"I want some armour," I said. "If we get hit, the pilot is the first to take damage. I don't have any armour to absorb it, so I'll be obliterated."

"We don't have any spare armour on board," Gary said.

"What about yours?" Max suggested.

Gary stared. "You're not serious?" he demanded.

"Well, if you think *you* can get us through this,

then..." I said, leaving the thought hanging and moving to sit back down.

"OK, OK!" shouted Gary. He pressed a button on his chest, causing his suit of armour to pop off then retract violently, until it was nothing but a miniaturised breastplate, about the size of a small handbag. Gary, now a few feet shorter and looking a lot less musclebound in a pair of space-themed boxer shorts, grudgingly handed the armour to me, at which point it expanded round my own body.

"WOAH!" shouted Max. "Flo, you're huge. You look like a superhero."

"I feel like one," I said, flexing my now-huge biceps.

"Yes, yes, you look very big and impressive," said Gary. "Now would you please get us out of here!"

"Oh right, yeah," I said, shoving past him to get into the cockpit. By now there were what looked like hundreds of ships outside, all shooting at each other. A quick glance at the Lightbringer's control deck told me that our shields were at critical level. One more shot and we were toast.

"First tanks, now spaceships," groaned Max, strapping himself into the co-pilot's seat next to me. "People in this game really need to find a way to communicate instead of shooting at each other all the time."

I yanked the flight stick, pulling the ship up just in time to avoid a blast that would have finished us off.

"*Nice moves, bro, but I'm still going to get you,*" came a voice.

"Who's that?" asked Max.

"That'll be the guy who just tried to blow us up," I said.

"How come we can hear other players anyway?" asked Max.

"*Star Smasher* has built-in Voice Chat," I explained.

Video Game Tip: Voice Chat is a great way for players from all over the world to quickly and easily insult each other.

GTVGT

Video Game Tip: Thankfully, it usually comes with a mute option.

I picked up the microphone. "I'm no bro, bro," I retorted, rounding the ship to face him. A couple of shots later, his ship exploded into a collection of brightly coloured pixels.

"Back to the nearest space station for him," I said. But there was no time to relax. When the explosion cleared, two other fighters emerged. Instead of retreating, I flew straight towards them, spinning the ship like a drill. In their rush to get out of the way, the two ships flew into each other, creating another spectacular burst of colour.

More shots from other ships rained down on us, but none of them hit. I twisted, turned, looped-the-loop,

dived, climbed, spun
and shook through the
laser blasts, firing back
my own more accurate
shots. It was like dancing.
Except with laser cannons.
And explosions. And spaceships. It was nothing like
dancing.

"Who's next?" I yelled over the microphone. But
most of the ships had come to a standstill.

"Ha!" I said, grinning at Max. "They're too scared
to come at me now."

"That was incredible," said a
wide-eyed Gary. "That was
the best piloting I've ever
seen. You saved my
life! I'm so sorry

about that whole Red Ghost thing."

"Thank you," I said.

A puzzled expression had formed on Max's face. He was staring at the console. "Um ... Flo ... what is that huge green blob on the radar?"

"What huge green blob?" I said, looking for myself. Sure enough, there it was. "Where did that come from... According to this it's now directly behind us."

I slowly rotated the ship until we were staring at the blob. It was the size of ten cruise liners, and it had appeared from nowhere. Its sides were bristling with laser cannons bigger than our ship. And they were all pointing at us.

LEVEL 6

"What *is* that?" cried Max.

"It's the *Phoenix*," said Gary and I together.

Max's eyes lit up. "You mean…"

"My dad's ship," explained Gary. "It's the crown jewel of the Imperial Fleet – the largest, grandest spaceship in the entire universe. It must have heard our distress call after all."

"It's very big," noted Max.

"It's also our ticket out of here," I whispered in his ear.

Our ship shuddered again.

"What was that?" asked Max. "Have we been hit?"

"No," I said, taking my hands off the flight stick. Our ship had started moving towards the *Phoenix*. "I think we're being beamed up."

Gary nodded. "Yeah, that'll be the new tractor beams Dad had installed. He's been itching to use them."

A huge panel in the side of the *Phoenix* slid open, revealing a large spacecraft hangar. As our ship floated into it, I realized I had been here before. Many times, in fact. I recognized the assortment of steel beams scattered randomly about the place, the smoke coming out of pipes for no obvious reasons and the odd faceless droid busily soldering the sides of a few half-built ships. The only difference was the army of three thousand soldiers carrying laser cannons and waiting for us.

"Oh yeah," said Gary, slapping his forehead, as

the ship touched down on a landing pad. "I totally forgot. They all still think you're the Red Ghost."

"Then correct them," I told him.

"Right, yes, of course," said Gary. He let out a long sigh. "Pity. Dad would have been so proud of me if I'd actually caught the real Red Ghost."

"Look, just be honest with him," I said. "Tell him you don't want to be a Space Soldier any more. I'm sure he'll understand."

"You really think so?" He hesitated. "Maybe you're right. Yes, that's what I'll do. Thank you, Flo."

Gary looked like he was about to hug me when the ship doors burst open, revealing several Space Soldiers, their laser cannons trained on me and Max.

"Outside!" barked the large soldier closest to us. "Nice and slowly. But quickly. But not too quickly. Move!"

"Bit grumpy, that one," said Max as we got up and followed Gary outside.

"That's Space Soldiers for you," said Gary. "They're always in a foul mood. To be fair, they spend ninety-nine per cent of their lives getting blown up by lasers, which would annoy me too."

We were led out of the hangar and along a marble corridor. Lining the walls were more Space Soldiers, each one carrying a bigger laser cannon than the last.

Eventually, after walking for what felt like a mile, we stopped outside a large golden door. Waiting in front of it was a tall, thin, slightly bored-looking man dressed in what appeared to be an armoured tuxedo.

"Ah, Henry, good to see you," said Gary. "This is Henry, Dad's right-hand man. Or left-hand man. It depends where he's standing."

"Your father is waiting for you in the imperial throne room," said Henry in a dull, monotonous voice. "He wants to see the Red Ghost with his own eyes."

I glared at Gary as he pushed open the door, but he gave me a look that said, "Don't worry, I'll handle it," so I kept my mouth shut.

"This is perfect," I whispered to Max as we stepped inside on to a glistening marble floor. "I never thought it would be this easy! The throne room is where they keep the Resurrection Gem. They're delivering us right to it. The gem is our ticket out of here."

"Yeah," muttered Max. "We just need to do something about the million soldiers watching our every move."

"Minor details," I said.

"Seriously, we need to come up with a... Wow, that's a lot of jewels!" cried Max, gazing open-mouthed at the golden walls adorned with rubies and emeralds. He was so in awe of our new surroundings that he almost walked into one of the many large pillars standing throughout the grand room.

My attention was drawn to the left-hand side of the room – a wall made entirely of glass. The

Phoenix never normally entered Combat Zones so most of the ships had gathered outside, clearly trying to see what was going on. "It's like being fish in an aquarium," I said.

Like seemingly everywhere else on the ship, the throne room was full of heavily armed, heavily armoured and heavily annoyed-looking Space Soldiers. Most of them were focused on us, but there were a handful over in one corner of the room, surrounding what I could just make out as being a glass case housing a pulsating orange jewel. The Resurrection Gem!

At the far end of the room, sitting on a jewel-encrusted golden throne, was a short white-haired man wearing a suit of golden armour with a black cape trailing regally behind him.

"Presenting Emperor Horatio Orioncloud,"

boomed Henry, "leader of the Thousand Galaxies, ruler

of the Fallen Stars, champion of the Celestial Wars—"

"Yes, yes, Henry, that's plenty," said the Emperor, before jumping up from his throne and rushing over to hug Gary. "My boy! Tell me, why is it every time I send you out on a mission, you come home in your underpants?"

Gary rolled his eyes. "It's not *every* time. It's happened like ... five times."

"This is your *sixth* mission," interjected Henry.

"Oh, never mind all that," said the Emperor. "You're the hero of the Empire. I knew you had it in you. Everyone thought you'd never make it as a Space Soldier but now look at you."

"Everyone thought that?" asked Gary, looking a bit downbeat.

"Oh yes, absolutely everyone," the Emperor assured him. "Henry said you were the worst Space Soldier he'd ever seen, didn't you, Henry?"

Henry gave a little cough. "Yes, Your Majesty."

"But here you are," continued the Emperor, "single-handedly capturing the Red Ghost. I'm so proud of you!"

Gary looked over at me. "Well ... actually, Dad," he said. "That's not completely true."

The Emperor's eyebrows rose. "Oh?" he said.

Gary shook his head. "No... That is ... I didn't do it single-handedly. My squad helped."

"WHAT?" said Max and I together.

The Emperor let out a belly laugh. "Ha! My boy! Not only is he the finest Space Soldier the Empire has ever seen, he's also the humblest. Recognizing the contributions of others – why, if that isn't the mark of a true leader, then I don't know what is. Now, which one is it, then? Neither of them looks particularly red. Or like a ghost."

"It's the girl," said Gary. "She's got a red dress on underneath, you see. I saw it before she stole my armour."

The Emperor nodded. "Ah, yes, of course."

"You lying weasel!" I shouted. "I saved your life!"

"What's she talking about, Gary?" asked the Emperor.

"Oh, I wouldn't listen to her," said Gary. "She'll say anything to get out of trouble."

Suddenly everyone's heads turned towards the window, where the ships that had been watching us were suddenly dashing off in all directions.

"What the...?" said the Emperor, marching over to take a look.

A series of bright flashes outside lit up the throne room. It was chaos at first, as ships scrambled to get away. It took a few moments before I could see what they were rushing to escape from. It was a single ship. A red one.

"Gary," said the Emperor quietly, as he stared out of the window. "If the Red Ghost is standing right here, would you kindly explain to me – WHO THE DEVIL IS OUT THERE?"

Gary laughed nervously. "Ah, yes ... funny story..."

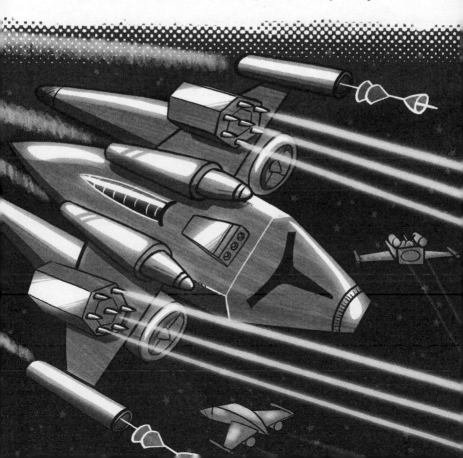

LEVEL 7

"I can explain," said Gary.

"I'm looking forward to this." I folded my arms.

"Yes, well, it'll have to wait a moment, won't it?" said the Emperor. "Henry, get every Space Soldier we have in a ship and send them out there. I want that Red Ghost taken care of, once and for all!"

"Yes, Your Majesty," said Henry. He made a gesture and within seconds the room was entirely cleared of Space Soldiers. Max and I shot knowing glances at each other and then towards the corner of the room, where the case containing the Resurrection

Gem was now unguarded.

"When you say *every* Space Soldier...?" asked Gary nervously.

"Don't worry, Gary, I didn't mean you," said the Emperor.

"Oh, thank goodness," said Gary.

"I meant REAL Space Soldiers," the Emperor snapped.

Gary's face fell flat. "Oh."

"I'm so disappointed in you," continued the Emperor. "To lie to my face like that. I don't know where I went wrong with you, I really don't. I did all the things a father is supposed to do for their child: I enrolled you in Space Soldier Nursery when you were just a baby. I made sure you went to the best Space Soldier schools. Then when you didn't get the grades you needed for Space Soldier University,

I threatened to blow them up unless they let you in. And for what? To end up with a son who abandons his squad in the middle of a mission. I bet you left them behind with the actual Red Ghost?"

"Well ... we weren't sure..." said Gary, his lips starting to quiver. I thought he was definitely about to cry, but instead his face hardened. "Dad, have you ever once stopped to think that maybe the reason I'm no good as a Space Soldier is because I don't want to be one?"

The Emperor screwed up his face. "Of course not," he said. "What kind of question is that? Why in Alpha Centauri wouldn't you want to be a Space Soldier? It's the only job there is. Besides Emperor. And *I'm* the Emperor."

Gary shook his head. "There could be others," he said. "Like acting."

Max nudged me and nodded towards the Resurrection Gem.

"We should do it now," he muttered. "While those two are busy arguing."

"Right," I said. Slowly we started shuffling sideways towards the gem, until it became clear that Gary and his dad were way too busy yelling at each other to notice us. Then we broke out into a full sprint.

Close up, I could see that the pulsating orange stone was shaped like a diamond but roughly the size of a pineapple. A sign above the case read: *In case of emergency break glass*. I looked at Max.

"I'd say being trapped inside a video game counts as an emergency," he said.

"Fair enough," I said, before punching a giant armoured hand through the glass, leaving the Resurrection Gem exposed.

"So we smash this weird glowing orange thing, and ... game over?" asked Max.

"Right," I said. "And hopefully we go home."

I reached down and picked up the gem. It wasn't as heavy as I expected it to be, but the light shining out of it made it difficult to look at directly. I lifted it above my head.

Just as I was about to bring it down, someone grabbed it from behind me, yanking it out of my hands.

"As if I don't have enough to deal with!" said the Emperor, clutching the gem to his chest. "The Empire under attack, finding out my son is a coward and now you two trying to smash the Resurrection Gem."

"No, you don't understand," I protested.

"Er ... Flo," said Max, pointing towards Gary. "What's going on with him?"

Gary's face had turned bright red.

"COWARD, AM I?" he yelled. "WOULD A COWARD DO THIS?"

Gary lunged towards his dad and tore the Resurrection Gem from his hands before bringing it crashing to the ground, where it smashed instantly in a huge surge of blinding orange light.

"NOOOOOOOO!" wailed the Emperor.

The light quickly faded, but that was the only thing to leave the room. Max and I hadn't gone anywhere.

"Gary, why would you do that?" asked the Emperor. "That's the last one we had in stock. We won't get any more in until Monday."

"Serves you right," said Gary, folding his arms.

"Wait a minute," I said. "Are you saying that you just ... keep replacing those things?"

The Emperor looked at me as if I'd asked if he thought space was a bit on the large side. "Of course we do," he said. "We usually replace it several times a day. Why else do you think it's called the Resurrection Gem?"

"Because it restores life to all your Space Soldiers," I said.

The Emperor screwed up his face. "Is that what people think?" he said, scratching his head. "Is that why we have Space Soldiers in here every day smashing the thing? I say Space Soldiers, but Henry has this curious theory that they're actually spies who've infiltrated the army to gain access to my throne room. He's forever trying to get me to update our recruitment policy... Anyway, no, it doesn't do that. It's just a nice light that I'm fond of, that's all. Our Space Soldiers come back to life, because ... because that's just how things work."

This wasn't good. I looked at Max who had slumped to the ground.

"Max..." I began.

"It's hopeless," he groaned. "We're going to be stuck here forever! Why couldn't we at least get stuck in a nice peaceful building game like *Blocktopia*? Or maybe a puzzle game? I love a good puzzle. Like anagrams. I'm really good at those."

"Pull yourself together, Max," I said.

"Truthful Alex employs ogre," said Max. "See? I can

make anagrams of anything!"

"All right, knock it off," I told him.

"Folk lick a fortnight," replied Max, before giggling to himself.

Just as I was about to tell Max to get up, the Emperor and Gary gasped. I turned round to see the small red fighter ship floating outside the window as if it was staring at us. There was no sign of any other ships out there. The battle was already over.

"The Red Ghost," I said quietly.

"The Red Ghost," repeated Max. "Rhett Hodges."

I turned my head slowly to Max. "What did you just say?"

But before Max could answer, the ship outside rotated until its door was directly in front of the throne-room window. Then the hatch slid open.

There he was. Rhett Hodges. Or his face anyway

– the image of a surly looking teenage boy, a black fringe taking up almost half of his face and a fixed sneer covering the rest, emblazoned upon the head of a crimson Space Soldier, wielding a large red laser cannon.

A question I should have asked a long time ago entered my head.

"I can see that he's red," I said. "But why the ghost part?"

I didn't have to wait long for the answer. Rhett leaped from his ship and passed straight through the window as if it wasn't there. He landed just a few feet from us.

The Red Ghost raised his weapon and blasted Max in the chest before doing the same to me.

LEVEL 8

"Hodges!" I yelled. "Hodges is the Red Ghost!
I always knew he was the kind of player to use
cheats. Jumping through walls? Classic hack. Hey ...
where are we?"

Max waved a hand around the grey, barren, crater-
filled landscape before adding, "You don't recognize
it?"

Max had missed the point. "Yeah, obviously I can
see we're back at the moon starting level," I said.
"But we shouldn't be. This game has checkpoints.
We were at the end level. We should have

respawned on the *Phoenix*. It doesn't make any sense... Unless... Of course! It must be another of Hodges' hacks."

Max shrugged. "What does it matter?" he asked. "We're not going home either way, are we?"

"Max, we can't lose hope," I said. "We will get out of here, I promise. We just need to find a way back to the *Phoenix* first."

Max didn't look very enthused. "Again?" He sighed. "I suppose we'll need another ship, then."

"Not a problem," I said. "I'll just steal a tank and see what I can rustle up."

"There are no tanks," said Max.

"No tanks?" I looked around the landscape. He was right. There wasn't a single one. "I don't get it. Where is everyone?"

"Gone, that's where," came a familiar voice.

We looked down into the crater next to us. At the bottom, slumped against the side, was Captain Moretta. Her helmet was lying next to her and she looked weary.

"Captain Moretta!" I exclaimed. "What happened?"

"The Red Ghost happened," she said, not bothering to raise her head. "I've never seen anything like it. He didn't even have to aim at his targets. He just fired and someone would blow up."

"Auto-aim," I mumbled to myself, adding it to the list of hacks Hodges had to be using.

"People would shoot back," continued Moretta. "But the shots that landed ... they'd just bounce off like they were nothing."

"No-damage," I murmured.

"It went on for ages," said Moretta. "Every time a tank got destroyed it'd respawn a few seconds later, only for the same thing to happen again. Eventually the tanks just stopped coming."

It was classic troll behaviour. Ruin the game for everyone else so no one wanted to play any more. I'd never seen it work as well as this, though.

"What happened to the rest of your squad?" asked Max. "Did you try to fight him?"

"No, he never saw us," she replied. "I ordered the squad to stay low and monitor the situation. But we must have gotten too close or something, because the Ghost fired a few shots and toasted everyone. Everyone but me. Maybe I was outside the automatic aiming range or something, I don't know. I'm just glad that my unit would have respawned back at the *Phoenix*, so at least they're safe now."

Max and I looked at each other. "No, they're not," I said. "He's at the *Phoenix* now. He took out the entire fleet by himself."

Captain Moretta leaped out of the crater. "He's at the *Phoenix*?" she shouted. "We have to stop him!"

"I don't know if we can," I said. "With those cheats he's using, he's invincible."

Captain Moretta considered this for a moment, then said, "All I know is that I'm tired of this war.

People show up. They blast us, or we blast them. They respawn. We respawn. Round and round we go forever. Somehow we need to find a way to break this endless cycle. We must find peace."

Max's eyes went as wide as some of the nearby craters. "Flo, I think that's it!" he exclaimed.

"What?"

"Breaking the cycle," he said. "What if that's how we get out of the game?"

"What does that even mean?" I asked.

"I don't know exactly," Max admitted. "But we tried to bring down the Emperor and that didn't work. What if we have to help him instead?"

"You mean by defeating Hodges?" I said. "But he's hacking. No one beats hackers, Max."

Max refused to accept that. "I bet you could," he said. "I mean, you are the best at this after all.

And you did beat him before..."

Max was clearly trying to flatter me, hoping that my need to be the best at this game would be enough to convince me that I could find a way to beat Hodges.

And ... well ... he was right.

"All right, I'm in," I said.

Even though our odds were still slimmer than a mushroom after being jumped on by a moustachioed plumber, the idea that not all hope was lost seemed to give Max a boost as he cheered.

"Let's do this," said Captain Moretta.

Caught up in the excitement, the three of us set off, before realizing something and stopping dead.

"We still need a ship," said Max.

"Yep," I agreed

"Please tell me Gary remembered to request

one?" said Moretta. There was a hint of hope in her voice, but not so much that it sounded confident.

"I ... can't remember," I admitted.

"Me neither," said Max.

"Ugh! I wish we were playing the game instead of being in it," I said. "We could have just used fast-travel."

Video Game Tip: Fast-travel lets you travel instantly between locations you've already visited. A bit like when you fall asleep during a long car journey then wake up when you get there, except without the sore neck.

I looked up into the star-filled sky and then, as if on cue, a small shape formed and rapidly grew larger. Seconds later, a transport ship landed next to us. A door slid open and a male voice shouted out, "Hey, Moretta, you need a lift?"

"Pete?" said Moretta. "Man, am I glad to see you."

The three of us piled on to the ship. While Moretta and Pete exchanged notes on the Red Ghost, something caught my eye outside the window. A new tank had spawned.

"Hey, look at that!" I said to Max. "I guess not everyone got the message to keep away."

Max looked over my shoulder. "They're not very good, though, are they?" he said.

Max was right, the newcomer really didn't seem to know what they were doing. After some erratic driving, their tank quickly became wedged in a small crater. Clearly the person had never played the game before, and didn't even know the basic controls. Hardly the sort of player who'd be any help stopping the Red Ghost. But it was a small reminder that Hodges hadn't won. Not yet, anyway.

LEVEL 9

Our second trip to the *Phoenix* proved a lot quieter than the first. Too quiet, really. Other than the Emperor's vessel itself, the only ship we could see was the red fighter belonging to Hodges, still parked outside the throne-room window.

"We'll take one of the service entrances," Pete said, flying us in low, beneath the *Phoenix*. He tapped a code into his dashboard and seconds later a small hatch opened in the huge ship's underside.

We came up into a long tunnel, motion-sensor lights activating as we flew along, illuminating the darkness. Eventually we arrived at a landing bay. There wasn't much there apart from a metal ladder that led out of the tunnel.

"That'll take us right to the throne room," said Pete.

Captain Moretta shook her head. "Not you, Pete," she said. "You're a pilot, not a fighter. You're not trained for this."

"*I'm* not trained for this," muttered Max.

Pete looked a bit disappointed but nodded. "I'll head back to the barracks, then," he said. "Wait for the others to respawn. I'll fill them in when they do."

The three of us got out and waved Pete off, before starting the climb towards the throne room.

Video Game Tip: Ladders in video games are a great way to travel between floors. There are typically three ways to use them: 1. Go up. 2. Go down. 3. Accidentally press the climb button too late and plummet helplessly to the ground.

"So the Space Soldiers don't instantly respawn?" asked Max as we clambered up the ladder.

"Sometimes they do," said Moretta. "Other times it can take half an hour or so. No one knows why, that's just the way it is."

I was pretty sure it was because the makers of the game wouldn't want thousands of characters respawning in the same location at once, so they just did a few at a time. But now didn't seem like the time to explain to Moretta about her being a character inside a video game.

"Shouldn't we wait, then?" asked Max. "For backup?"

"It won't help us," I said. "If Hodges sees an army, he'll just blast them. I think to beat him, we need to keep it small."

"So you've got a plan?" asked Moretta.

"Maybe," I said. The quiet ride back to the *Phoenix* had given me time to think about how we could stop Hodges. Thanks to his hacks, he could blast us without even trying, so we had to get that laser cannon off him. Normally it wouldn't be possible in the game to disarm another player. But I realized that like Hodges, Max and I didn't have to play by the rules either. Even so, it wasn't going to be easy.

After several minutes of climbing, Moretta finally stopped and led us out into a dark, cramped passage. When we reached the end she shoved open a rusting door that led to the corridor outside the throne room.

"Is there any other way in?" I asked.

She considered. "There's an air vent that comes out behind the Emperor's throne."

"That's perfect," I said.

"But it's too small for anyone wearing armour to fit through," she warned. We both looked at Max.

"Oh, great," he said.

"This is your chance to be the hero," I told him. "I'm going to keep Hodges distracted. All you have to do is drop down when I give the signal and snatch his laser cannon."

Max looked flabbergasted. "Oh, is THAT all?" he

said sarcastically, before sighing. It was a sigh that I'd heard hundreds of times before, always right after I asked him to do something that could be considered a "bad" idea. That's how I knew he was going to do it.

"What's the signal?" asked Moretta.

"When I say 'game over,'" I said.

Moretta put a hand on Max's shoulder. "Come on, I'll show you where it is."

"How are you going to keep him distracted?" Max asked me.

"By giving him exactly what all trolls want," I said.

"What's that?"

"The chance to show someone how clever they are," I said, before kicking open the throne-room door.

LEVEL 10

Standing next to the throne, Hodges raised his laser cannon.

"Stop!" I shouted, throwing my hands up. "I just want to talk."

Hodges held his fire. "Florence Waters?" he said. "It is you! Hang on, I sent you back to the start. How did you get here so quickly?"

"It's Flo, actually," I said. "And I speedrun this game all the time. If anything I'm slower than usual."

Video Game Tip: Speedrunning is a way of playing games where the goal is to finish it in as fast a time as possible, like a race or your homework.

"Right after I blasted you, I thought, wasn't that Florence Waters?" he continued. "But how on Earth did you get your hands on a DIS? There's no way your mum could afford one on a government salary. You didn't steal one, did you? That's wrong, you know."

"No!" I snapped. "I mean, yes, it's wrong. But no, I never stole one. If you must know, my mum's a genius. She built one herself."

Hodges gave a forced laugh. "Genius, ha! If anyone's a genius, it's me. But actually, you being here is perfect. Come in, come in."

I took a few tentative steps towards Hodges. It was then that I noticed the Emperor and Gary standing together in the corner.

"Waters, have you seen this?" said Hodges, turning towards them. "I don't remember the NPCs being so intelligent."

I looked again at the Emperor and Gary, still in his space-themed underwear. "Intelligent?" I said. "Really?"

"That's enough cheek from you, young lady," said the Emperor. "As if I didn't have enough on my plate without this jumped-up little popinjay taking out my entire army."

Hodges burst into laughter. "Popinjay! Who talks like that? Classic. But you see what I mean, Waters? It's like they're actually capable of talking to us. The makers must have released a new update or something. It's a pity I'm going to make sure no one ever plays this game again."

"Why?" I asked.

"Why?" he repeated. "WHY? Isn't it obvious?"

"Um ... no. Why don't you explain it for me?"

I said, stealing a glance at the ceiling. I could see the grate covering the air vent that Max was hopefully crawling through. I could only hope that Hodges' explanation was long enough to give Max time to reach it.

"Why don't you cast your mind back to last month?" said Hodges. "It was a simpler time. One where I ruled the universe of *Star Smasher*, fair and square. Thousands of people would watch me play every day. I had it all. Fame, glory, money. The best player this game had ever seen. I never lost a contest. And then, one fateful stream, in player-versus-player ship combat, I came across a small, harmless-looking fighter ship. You. It should have been an easy kill, you in your tiny fighter, me in my fully kitted-out war machine."

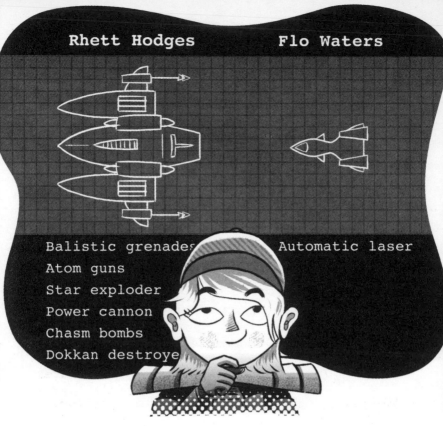

Balistic grenades   Automatic laser
Atom guns
Star exploder
Power cannon
Chasm bombs
Dokkan destroye

I smiled, remembering how it had played out. It was up there with my all-time favourite moments.

"Everyone thought they had to have the biggest, baddest guns to beat you," I said. "But you already had those. What no one else realized was that all those weapons slowed your ship down. I knew the best shot at beating you was to come at you in the lightest, fastest ship possible."

Hodges' laser cannon swung towards me. I thought he was going to shoot, but then he lowered it again and turned his back to me.

"It was humiliating," he said. "Thankfully no one was able to see the moment when you finally defeated me..."

"That's because you stopped streaming," I said.

At that moment, something caught my eye. It was Moretta creeping into the room. She gave me the briefest of nods, which I took to mean Max had got into the vent OK, before she slipped behind one of the marble pillars.

"Of course I cut the stream," said Hodges. "I had to protect my reputation as the number one *Star Smasher* player in the world. But ... it backfired."

No one believed it was an accident. Most of my subscribers abandoned me after that because nobody wants to watch someone who can't even beat a little girl."

I almost exploded at that point, but somehow managed to stop myself. "Maybe," I said through gritted teeth, "they just didn't want to watch someone who throws a temper tantrum when he gets beaten fair and square?"

"How are you making your character go so red in the face?" he asked, ignoring my question. "The Imprint Scanner you stole must be some serious piece of tech. Much better than mine."

"I told you, I didn't steal it," I said.

"Sure you didn't," he said sarcastically. "Just like you didn't steal my career. It's your fault, you know. You left me with no choice."

I considered this for a moment. "You mean no choice but to spend lots of time practising, get better at the game then come back and beat me?" I asked.

There was a long pause. "No," he said eventually. "I mean to use every cheat and hack I could come up with to tear this game down and make sure no one ever wants to play it again. Then I'm guaranteed to be the greatest player of all time."

I couldn't believe what I was hearing. "That doesn't make any sense!" I said. "You love this game. You'd honestly rather have no one ever play it again than not be the best at it?"

"I wouldn't expect someone like you to understand," he said, his anger starting to show. "You don't know what it's like to be truly great at something."

I glanced up at the vent cover. I had to hope Max
was in position. I wouldn't be able to stall Hodges
for much longer.

"But why hasn't anyone reported you?" I asked.
"It's obvious you're using cheats. The people
running the game should have banned you ages
ago. I mean, you're even going about with your own

face, for crying out loud!"

Hodges laughed. "See, this is what I'm talking about. You don't understand greatness. Do you think I'd be happy with just being some common troll using a few cheap hacks? I'm an artist. My hacks are more than just jumping through walls. Anyone can do that. You think they're not trying to ban me? They *can't* ban me!"

"What?" I said. "How is that even possible?"

"Because I'm the greatest hacker who ever lived," he said triumphantly. "And I want the world to know. The makers of the game can't get round my hacks to kick me from the game. It'd take a genius to disable them."

"A ... genius?" I asked, freezing. Something occurred to me. Of course! How could I have missed it! The solution had been right in front of me. I knew how to stop Hodges for good.

"Enough," I said. "It's GAME OVER."

I stood there, waiting for Max to appear. Nothing. Gary and the Emperor looked at me with the same puzzled expression.

"I said, it's GAME OVER!"

"Yes, I heard you," said Hodges. "Am I meant to be scared or something?"

I looked up at the ceiling. Max had surely had enough time to crawl through the vent. Unless ... he couldn't get the grate open.

Moretta must have had the same thought because at that moment she leaped out from behind the column and fired a blast above Hodges' head, blowing the grate off.

"What a lousy shot," said Hodges. He fired a single blast back at Moretta, who instantly disappeared.

"Moretta, no!" shouted Gary.

Hodges spun round. "Ha, I'd forgotten about you two," he said, pointing his laser cannon towards them. It was then that Max dropped from the ceiling, landing on Hodges with a thud.

"What the...?" shouted Hodges, but before he could get to his feet, Max had seized the laser cannon and tossed it to me.

Hodges sprang back up. "How did you do that?" he demanded, looking at Max. "I've never seen anyone disarm another player before. But if you think that's going to stop me, you're sadly mistaken."

Another laser cannon suddenly appeared in Hodges' hands.

"Oh, come on!" shouted Max.

"I told you I was the greatest," laughed Hodges, firing a shot towards the Emperor. But it wasn't the Emperor who got hit. In his space-themed boxer shorts, Gary threw himself in front of his dad, taking the entire blast and vanishing.

The Emperor let out a roar.

I raised the laser cannon in my arms and fired. The ray struck Max in the chest, and he was gone.

"You missed too," laughed Hodges. "I'm surrounded by lousy shots."

"I wasn't aiming for you," I said, before firing the laser cannon at myself.

LEVEL 11

"What did you do that for?" yelled Max as we regenerated back on the starting moon, thanks to Hodges' laser-cannon hack.

"You trust me, right?" I asked.

Max thought about this for less than a second. "You just shot me with a laser," he said, "and before that you got me stuck inside a video game!"

"I'm going to take that as a 'yes'," I replied, walking past him.

"Flo, what's going on?" asked Max.

"I have a hunch," I said. I could see the worried

expression on his face. "No, it's more than a hunch. I'm sure I'm right. Just come with me."

I hurried across the moon's surface and was glad to hear Max's footsteps behind me moments later. Luckily what I was looking for was still there, stuck in the same crater. Though now it was upside down for some reason.

"Is that the tank from earlier?" asked Max. "The one we saw from Pete's ship?"

I nodded. But if I was right, it was much more than that. I tapped on the outside of the tank. "Mum?"

"FLO!" shouted a voice from inside the tank. "Is that really you?"

"It's me, Mum!" I said.

"Thank goodness I found you," she said. "Or ... I suppose you found me, didn't you. Thank goodness either way!"

Max opened his mouth in shock. "Miss Waters, you used the device too?"

"Oh, hello, Max," said Mum sweetly. "No, dear, I didn't. I'd have to be quite foolish to use an untested device, especially after someone had gone to the trouble of leaving dozens of notes warning me not to use it, wouldn't I?"

Neither of us replied.

"I'm going to assume from this silence," continued Mum, "that both of you are very sorry?"

"Yes, Miss Waters/Mum," said Max and I together.

"To be fair, though, Mum," I said. "It's not like we could have expected *this* to happen, is it?"

Mum cleared her throat. "All right, yes, I'm probably not entirely blameless there," she admitted. "When you asked me to build a device to scan your image and turn it into a playable character I realized that we were basically doing something similar in my latest research project. For confidentiality reasons I can't tell you what that is. All I can say is that it involves breaking down the building blocks of a human being, turning them into computer code and then restoring them somewhere else."

"You're building a teleporter?" asked Max.

"What? How? I mean ... no," said Mum.

"It's pretty obviously a teleporter," I agreed.

"Fine, I'm building a teleporter," said Mum. "I smuggled home a prototype version so I could modify it to take a copy of someone. But I hadn't finished it, OBVIOUSLY! I still had to remove the parts that broke down the physical version of you. I'd just finished a cup of tea and was on my way upstairs to fix it. I hadn't heard any noise from your room in a while so I went to have a look. Of course, you weren't there, which led me to check my workshop, where I saw this game playing on the monitor. That's when I realized that the device had restored you both into this game. So I picked up a controller and joined the game to try to find you."

Max and I looked at each other and I could tell we were both thinking the same thing. Mum could easily have come across the game and figured we'd just forgotten to turn it off. Then she might have switched it off herself. I didn't want to think too much about what might have happened to us after that.

"Can someone please help me out of this silly contraption?" said Mum. "I've pressed all the keys. Darling, I have seven degrees, three PhDs, a Nobel Prize and a *Pointless* Trophy – this shouldn't be so difficult!"

"Press *E*," I said.

There was a brief, slightly awkward pause, then Mum appeared next to us. Well, not Mum exactly. She must have joined the game using my avatar, so Max and I were looking up at an eight-foot-tall, chrome-armoured Space Soldier. I definitely didn't want to find out what happened if I ignored this version of Mum's signs.

"OK, maybe I didn't press *all* the keys, then. Thank you," said Mum. "Now, about getting you out of here. I've been running calculations and it looks like your best chance of escaping the game is to—"

"Complete it," I finished. "Yeah, that's what we thought."

"I see," said Mum, sounding a little annoyed. "You really can't help yourself jumping in before I've finished today, can you?"

"Sorry, Mum," I said, grinning.

"Yes, well," she continued. "The problem is that the game now has a lock on you both. I've been examining the code behind it and I believe that the only way to release that lock safely is for you to, like you say, complete the game."

Max turned to me. "How did you know it was your mum?"

"It was Hodges," I said. "When he talked about needing a genius to beat him, I immediately thought of Mum."

"Aww, sweetheart, how nice of you," said Mum.

"Then for some reason that made me think of the tank we saw from the ship," I added, "and how whoever was controlling it was clearly hopeless at games. Because Mum is like the worst video game player ever."

"Hmm," sniffed Mum. "Not quite as flattering, that one."

"And then I realized it *had* to be Mum," I said. "Hodges has run everyone else off, but Mum would come looking for us."

"Who is this Hodges you keep mentioning?" asked Mum.

Max and I filled her in on everything that had happened since we arrived in the game.

"Wow, the Emperor and his son sure do seem to have a lot of issues to work out," said Mum, once we were done.

"What about Hodges?" I said. "Do you think you can remove his hacks?"

"Oh yeah, sorry, sweetheart, I disabled them ages ago," she said. "During the bit about the space battle."

"Mum, you're amazing!" I exclaimed. "Now we need to get back to the ship and stop him for good."

"How are we going to do that?" asked Max. "We don't have a ship."

I smiled. "We don't need one," I said. "Mum, press *Shift*, *P* and *3*. No ... Mum, that's the 'crouch' key. *Shift* and ... No, you're jumping now. MUM! *SHIFT*, *P*, *3*. That's it!"

There was a chime and the three of us glowed bright yellow for a second. Max began to grow as chrome armour formed round him while my own suit changed colour to match the others.

Laser cannons appeared, strapped to our backs.

"Finally!" said a delighted Max, flexing his new-found muscles. "But how?"

"Mum's just formed a group," I said. "It's a feature of *Star Smasher* for friends to team up. Everyone gets the same equipment and it also allows us to fast-travel. Mum, I'll need you to follow my instructions carefully. And when we get to the ship there are a few more commands you'll need to learn..."

LEVEL 12

We reappeared outside the throne room to, once again, find ourselves staring down the wrong end of a laser cannon. But not just one. Hundreds. The corridor was full of angry-looking Space Soldiers. Max and I raised our arms. Mum started jumping on the spot.

Captain Moretta, Gary and Henry stepped through the crowd. "Lower your weapons, they're with us," said Moretta.

"Er ... yes, that's right, laser cannons down," added Gary.

"Nice armour," said Moretta. "Who's your friend?"

"Oh, that's my mum," I told her. "Mum, stop jumping, you're embarrassing me in front of the Space Soldiers."

"Sorry, dear," Mum apologized.

"What are you guys doing out here?" asked Max.

"Trying to come up with a plan," said Moretta. "The Red Ghost ... I mean Hodges is holding the Emperor hostage in there."

"If he'd simply blasted the Emperor," said Henry in his dull voice, "at least he'd respawn elsewhere and we could all get out of here. Instead, the Red Ghost is keeping him alive and terrorizing him."

"A few of us have tried to get in to rescue him," added Moretta, "but Hodges just keeps blasting us. We weren't sure if you two were coming back."

"Oh, we're back," I said. "And we're about to bring Hodges down for good."

"You'll save my dad?" asked Gary.

I shot Gary a look of disgust, remembering how he'd tried to pass me off as the Red Ghost to impress the Emperor.

"Look, I'm sorry," he said, staring at the ground. "I shouldn't have lied to my dad, especially after all you did for me. It's just ... I never feel like I'm good enough for him. He wants me to be interested in the same things he's interested in, and I'm not. I was just tired of being a disappointment to him."

I looked at Mum, who had obviously found the key that made your character lie down since she was currently sprawled on the floor. I realized how lucky I was to have a parent who, even though she clearly had no interest in games herself, knew how much I enjoyed them and encouraged that. OK, so building a machine that put me inside one of the games was probably going a bit far but still, her heart was in the right place.

"All right, Gary," I said. "Apology accepted. One question, though: why are you still wearing your boxer shorts? Wouldn't you have regenerated with new armour?"

"Yes," admitted Gary. "But to be honest, I've never found that armour very comfortable. This is much more freeing."

"Riiiiight," I said. "Max, Mum ... Mum, get up off the floor. *X*, Mum, press *X*. That's it. Let's do this."

I shoved open the door and the three of us walked back into the throne room. Hodges was casually firing laser blasts at the Emperor's feet, forcing him to hop around to avoid them. I realized he must have switched off auto-aim as he didn't seem concerned that his shots were missing.

"Oh, it's you again," said Hodges. "I thought it might be another of those Space Soldiers, come to rescue their emperor. It really is incredible you know... It's as if they actually care about this silly old man."

"Old man?" boomed the Emperor. "I'm only six hundred and five!"

"Leave him alone, Hodges," I said. "It's over."

"Oh, really," said Hodges. "Who says? You? Who's your new friend by the way? And why do they keep running into that pillar?"

"Mum, stop ... just... Max, can you help her?"

"Sure," said Max, rushing over to readjust Mum.

"I don't know why you bothered coming back," said Hodges. "Everyone else seems to have got the message. This game is mine now. Anyone who tries to play it will deal with me and... Wait a second ... you got back here in minutes. No one can speedrun this game that fast, not even me. Looks like I'm not the only one using hacks. You know what, though? No one is fast enough to beat my auto-aim."

There was an ominous click, which could only have been Hodges re-enabling his auto-aim hack. He raised his laser cannon at me and fired. I ducked and watched as the blast took out a chunk of the pillar behind me.

There was silence in the room. Hodges didn't move. The face of his avatar remained the same, but I would have given anything to be able to see his real one as it dawned on him what had just happened. It was the Emperor who spelled it out for him.

"He missed!"

"I... How... I don't... That's impossible," said Hodges, a tremble in his voice.

The Emperor didn't miss a beat, shoving Hodges aside and snatching his laser cannon. "I'll take that, you good-for-nothing scoundrel."

At this, some of the Space Soldiers started racing into the room. I could see Moretta and Gary among them.

"Wait, what's happening?" demanded Hodges, backing off. "How could I miss? And why can't I make another laser cannon appear? What's happened to my hacks?"

"We turned them off," I said. "Well, my mum did. You see that Space Soldier over there? That's her, and unlike you, she actually is a genius."

Mum suddenly fired a blast that almost took

off Hodges' head.

"Oops, sorry!" shouted Mum. "I was trying to wave. What's the key for waving?"

"There is no key for waving, Mum," I said, rolling my eyes.

Video Game Tip: Many games do now let you wave at other players. That's nice, eh?

"She's a genius at *other* things," I continued. "She's removed all your hacks for a start. Including the ones that stop them being able to ban you. And just to make sure they get to it quickly, I talked Mum through how to report a player for bad behaviour."

"I'll ... I'll ... just come back with a new account, then," said Hodges defiantly. "With new hacks. Better ones."

"Oh no, I don't think you will," said Mum. "For two reasons. One, I've supplied the makers of the game with your computer's address, so they'll be able to deactivate this and any other accounts you try to make."

"Or already have," I said, grinning.

"You mean … I'll lose my original account," he said, sounding horrified. "But it's got all my stats. It's the proof that I'm the best!"

"*Were* the best," I corrected.

"You said there were two reasons he wouldn't be able to make a new account…" said Max.

"That's right," said Mum. "The other is that Flo has helpfully told me where you live, so I'll be paying your mother a visit later on to let her know what you've been up to."

"NOOOOOOOOOOOOOO!" wailed Hodges. Then the red armour of his suit started flickering, his face becoming distorted as a strange, booming voice declared:

And with that, Hodges vanished. The Space Soldiers erupted into cheers.

Max and I looked at each other. The Red Ghost was gone, but we were still here.

"I don't get it," I said, as he and Mum joined me. "Surely that's enough to complete the game? What more could we possibly have to do?"

But before I could respond, the Emperor rushed over and threw his arms round us. "You did it," he said. "You three have rid us of our greatest enemy. How can I ever thank you?"

As I tried to think of an answer, Max beat me to it. "I've got an idea," he said. "Does everyone really have to be a Space Soldier?"

To my surprise, the Emperor appeared to consider the request. After a few moments, he looked over at Gary. "My boy," he said. "You saved me. You proved how brave you were, and that's the defining quality of a Space Soldier."

"You don't have to be a Space Soldier to be brave, Dad," said Gary.

The Emperor nodded thoughtfully. "I suppose so. And what about the rest of you?"

There was silence, until Captain Moretta spoke. "I've always been good at painting…"

"And I've long harboured a dream of getting into the asteroid-mining game, Your Majesty," said Henry.

"I reckon I'd make a pretty decent moon farmer," came another voice.

"I'm sick of flying people everywhere and never getting to have any fun myself," said Pete, the pilot from earlier. "I'd quite like to have a go at being a Space Soldier."

The Emperor stroked his beard pensively. "First of all," he said, "I think what we might need is someone to help figure out how to get people into all these new jobs. I don't suppose anyone has ever dreamed about being – what would you even call it – a careers advisor?"

A couple of hands shot up.

"Ah! Excellent," said the Emperor. "You know, maybe I have been wrong all these years. Maybe it's time the Empire branched out a little. Hmmmm, yes, what a great idea of mine. New jobs for everyone!"

The soon-to-be ex-Space Soldiers, and Pete, let out another almighty cheer.

"Now, Gary," said the Emperor, putting his arm round his son. "I think I would very much like to see one of these plays of yours. Tell me, are there any about kings or emperors?"

"I think there might be one or two..." said Gary.

"Splendid!"

As we watched them walk off, I heard a gasp at my side.

"Flo, you're fading," said Mum.

I held up my hands. She was right. I could already see through them. The same thing was happening to Max.

"We must have done it!" he exclaimed. "We completed the game. Flo, this means we're going home!"

"Yeah," I said, looking hopefully at Mum. "Right, Mum?"

"Yes..." she agreed, "... maybe."

"Maybe?" Max and I echoed together.

"Probably," said Mum, trying to sound more reassuring.

"Probably?" I repeated. My hands had completely disappeared now and the rest of me was going the same way. "Mum, tell us – what else could happen? Quickly!"

"Well, if you don't jump out of *Star Smasher*," she said, "then I suppose it's possible the game could just reset with you in it."

Max let out a moan. "You mean we might have to do this all over again?"

Mum didn't look convinced. "It's possible, though I doubt it," she said. "But something that does concern me slightly is that this game was launched inside a Game Library application."

"*G-Locker*," I said. "It stores all my games."

Mum nodded. "Yes, and while I think it quite unlikely, there is the chance that instead of simply jumping out of this game, you might in fact jump into—"

Mum's voice cut out abruptly as the entire world turned black. All I could see was Max next to me ... and there, in front of us, in giant neon green letters, the words:

BONUS LEVEL

I woke up with a jolt. I tried to look around but the room was in total darkness. I was definitely in bed. My bed? Was this my room? Why did my head feel so heavy?

Everything started coming back to me. Mum's device, entering the video game with Max, the tanks, the spaceships, Rhett 'the Red Ghost' Hodges, Gary and his dad the Emperor.

Had it all been a dream?

I let out a groan. *Of course* it had been a dream. You can't get sucked into a video game. It had seemed so real at the time, but dreams always do, don't they? And then you wake up and they quickly fade from your mind.

I couldn't help feeling a little cheated.

Although it had to be said, this dream didn't seem to be fading that quickly.

"Flo? Are you there?"

It was Max. I tried to remember if Max had been allowed to stay over last night, and couldn't. "Max?" I said. "Where are you?"

"Um, in bed, I guess," he said. "My head feels like a brick, by the way. It's like I've still got that space armour on."

"Space ... armour?" I repeated. Before I could ask him anything else there came a knock on the door.

"Who's that?" asked Max.

"It must be Mum," I said, pulling myself out of bed.

My legs felt weird, almost like they'd been encased in cement. In fact, my entire body did.

"I can't see anything," said Max. "Can you put on the light?"

"Er ... yeah, sure," I said, slowly moving towards the place where the knocking sound had come from and trying not to trip over anything in the process.

"OW!" I shouted.

"What is it?" asked Max.

"I just walked into the wall," I said. I ran my hands over it and found something small sticking out. "On the plus side, I think I've found the light switch."

I clicked the switch and let out a scream that was immediately echoed by Max. Or something that looked kind of like Max, except...

"You're made of bricks!" I screamed.

"So are you!" he yelled back.

That was when I realized this wasn't my bedroom. We were in some kind of cabin made from wooden-looking blocks. Without thinking, I opened the front door. Standing outside in the moonlight was a green, scaly, tentacled monster made entirely from bricks.

Max and I looked at each other.

"ARRRRRRGHHHHHHHHH!"

To be continued...